Try it again, Sam

Safety When You Walk

by JUDITH VIORST

PAUL GALDONE drew the pictures

Lothrop, Lee & Shepard Company • New York

E

For Jessie Klein, the perfect teacher

3/71

His name was Sam and what he wanted most in the whole world was to go somewhere all by himself—without his mother walking him there, or his father, or his big bossy sister Jennifer. "We'll let you try it one of these days," his mother always said. But it was never one of these days.

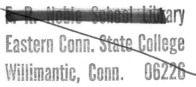

And then, one day, it was.

On Saturday, after breakfast, Sam's friend David called him on the telephone to invite him to play. Sam's mother said everyone was much too busy to take him, and *then* she said, "You know how to get there, Sam, and it isn't far away. How would you like to walk to David's house all by yourself?"

Sam said he positively would. He ran down the hall and was almost out the door when his mother stopped him. "Just a minute, Sam," she said.

Then Sam's mother told him to watch out for cars and pay attention to traffic lights and look where he was going and all that. "Yes," Sam said. "Yes, yes, yes." He squirmed and wiggled and scratched an itch on his shoulder. Oh, how he wanted to get started. But his mother was still talking. What was that she'd just said?

She said it once more. "I really mean it, Sam. If you get into any trouble on your way to David's, I expect you to turn right around and come back home. Is that a promise?"

Sam could tell his mother was very serious. He tried to be serious too. "Cross my heart and hope to die, stick a needle in my eye," said Sam.

His mother bent down and gave him a good-bye kiss. "Have a nice walk," she said. "And be careful."

"Yes," Sam said. "Yes, yes, yes." And he walked out the door very slowly, to show just how careful he was going to be.

Sam strolled down Union Street. He whistled *I've Been Working on the Railroad* and he tried not to step on any cracks in the sidewalk. He was feeling finer than fine.

Sam strolled past Harry Lee's house. Harry was out in front, bouncing a ball. "Thirty-seven, thirty-eight," counted Harry Lee. "Hi, Sam. I'm seeing how long—forty-four, forty-five—I can bounce."

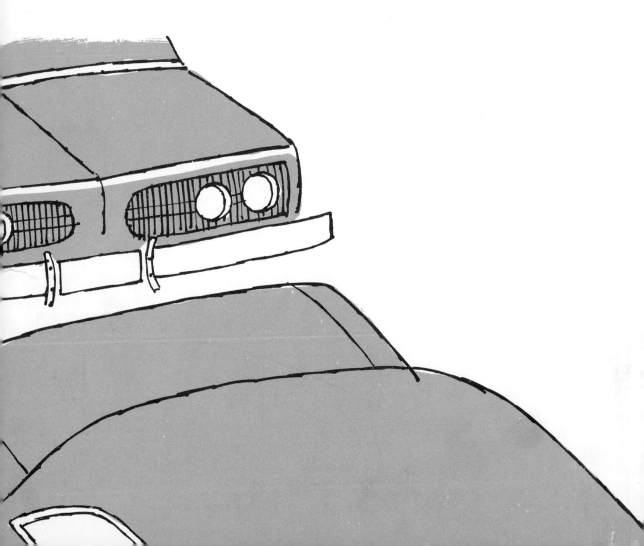

Sam watched Harry Lee bouncing and counting. "I'm going to David's house all by myself," he told him.

Harry Lee bounced up to sixty-two before he missed. Sam said he bet he could beat him. But when Sam bounced to forty-one, the ball hit a stone and rolled into the street.

Sam squeezed between two parked cars and ran after it.

Screech! A little red car stopped, almost on top of Sam.
A man jumped out and started yelling. He yelled things
about knuckleheaded kids who pop into streets from out of
nowhere. Then he jumped back into the little red car and
drove off.

Sam handed the ball to Harry Lee and walked on. But after a minute or two he remembered something. His mother had said, "If you get into any trouble on your way to David's, I expect you to turn right around and come back home." And he had cross-his-heart-and-hope-to-die promised that he would.

So Sam turned around. He didn't try not to step on the cracks in the sidewalk, and he didn't whistle anything at all.

When Sam got to his house he rang the bell even though the door wasn't locked, because he felt too sad to open the door by himself. "Why, Sam," his mother said when she let him in. "What happened?" And Sam told her.

His mother sighed and shook her head and scolded. But after a while she stopped her scolding and said, "I don't think you'll run in the street after balls anymore. And I know if you get into trouble you'll come back home. So if you still want to go to David's all by yourself,

you can try it again, Sam."

Sam quit being sad. He said another good-bye and walked off down the street and he didn't stop until he reached the corner. Something important was going to happen now. He was going to cross Calvert Avenue all by himself. He was going to cross as soon as the light turned green.

Sam leaned against the mailbox and waited for the green light. But the light stayed red. He waited and waited and waited. It still stayed red. He walked around the mailbox and kicked it a couple of times and then he looked up at the light. Red!

Sam thought he would burst if he waited another second.

"I'll run across fast," he decided, "faster than a rocket."

He hopped off the curb and started running. He ran so fast he didn't notice that a milk truck was turning the corner. He ran so fast he didn't notice that his shoelace had come undone. He didn't notice anything until he tripped on his shoelace and fell—smack in the middle of Calvert Avenue.

Bee-eee-eep! The milk truck was beeping its horn at Sam. It sounded angry. *Beep, beep, beep, beep!* Four more cars stood behind the milk truck and they sounded angry too. Sam tried to tie his shoelace faster than a rocket, but the beeping of the horns mixed him up.

At last Sam tied his shoe. He stood up and looked at the
other side of the street, the side he was trying to reach.
And then he turned around and went back the way he
had come, all the way back to his house.

Sam's mother was fixing lunch in the kitchen. "Oh, Sam," was all she said when he told her what had happened. But the way she said it made Sam sniff a long, noisy sniffle of shame.

Sam's mother gave him a tissue. She could see how sorry he was. "Wash your hands," she told him, "and have some lunch. And after you eat, well . . .

you can try it again, Sam."

Sam was so happy he ate two peanut-butter-and-jellies, and a glass of milk, and chocolate pudding with cream, and five Lorna Doones. He was so happy that he didn't even argue when his mother said to take an umbrella because it might rain. "See you later, mashed potater," he said.

Sam walked to the corner,
waited for the light to turn
green, and crossed just right—
not too slow and not too fast.
At last he was on the other side.

Splash. A drop of rain bounced off Sam's nose. Another
hit his shoe. Sam opened the umbrella. It was round on
top and it looked like a deep, dark cave. Sam couldn't
see a thing. I'm trapped, he said to himself as he walked
up Calvert Avenue. I'm trapped in a deep, dark cave.

"Ooo! Ow!" Sam had bumped into somebody, but he couldn't see who the somebody was. "Ow! Ooo!" That sounded like a voice he knew. Slowly Sam lifted the umbrella and peeked out. And there, rubbing her arm and jumping up and down on one foot and making a horrible fuss, was his big bossy sister Jennifer.

"Hi, Jen," Sam said in a squeaky little voice. "I'm going to David's house all by myself."

"You jerk!" screeched Jennifer. "You couldn't go to the *living room* all by yourself. I'm telling Mother on you—this minute."

"Never mind," Sam sighed. "*I'll* tell her."

Sam's mother listened to Jennifer say that Sam ought to be locked in a cage until he was at least twenty-one and she listened to Sam beg for another chance. "We'll see," she told him. "It's too wet outside to go anywhere right now. If the rain stops later this afternoon,

you can try it again, Sam."

Sam sat down by the window and muttered "Rain, rain, go away" over and over and over again. Sometimes saying it worked and sometimes it didn't. This time it did.

Sam said good-bye, walked to the corner, waited for the light, crossed just right, and turned up Calvert Avenue to Grant Street. At the corner of Grant he saw an old empty house with a "No Trespassing" sign and boards where the windows used to be. Some boys were peeking out.

"Come on in," they called to Sam,
"we're finding treasures."
Sam couldn't say no to treasures.
He started up the stairs.

One step. Two steps. Three steps. Four. . . . Suddenly there was a terrible *cru-uh-uh-unch*. The fourth step broke into splinters and fell away, carrying Sam with it. When the dust had settled, nothing could be seen of Sam except his arms, his shoulders, and his face.

Sam climbed out. He was covered with dust from head to toe, and he felt very gloomy indeed. "Find your own treasures," he said to the boys. "I've got to go home."

Sam's mother was baking a cake for dinner. When Sam walked in, her mixing bowl clattered to the floor. It took Sam a long time to explain about the dust, and longer than that to help mop up the cake batter, and even longer than that to convince his mother to let him have one last chance. But finally she said, "All right,

you can try it again, Sam."

Before she could take it back, Sam gave her a hug and
walked down to the corner, across the street, up
Calvert, and over to Grant, as careful as a person could be.
On he went down Grant Street, on to High's Bakery at the
other end of the block. David's house was just across from
High's. And there was David, sitting on his stoop. "Hurry
up, Sam," he hollered.

But Sam was waiting for the light to change. He waited
and waited and waited. He walked around the trash can.
He sang *Bobby Shafto* and whistled *I've Been Working on
the Railroad* and recited the alphabet—first frontwards
and then backwards. The light turned green.

Sam lifted his foot off the curb. "Just a minute, Sam," said someone in a loud voice. It was nosy Mrs. High from the bakery. "I'm going your way," she said to Sam. "I'll walk you across."

Mrs. High snatched Sam's hand and held it firmly in hers. "Please," begged Sam, trying to wriggle free. "I'm going to David's house all by myself—and I don't need any help."

"Nonsense," said Mrs. High. "Now come along."

But Sam didn't want to come along. He pressed his feet into the pavement and tried to weigh a thousand pounds. Mrs. High tugged. Sam pressed his feet some more. The light turned red.

Sam thought about giving Mrs. High a little kick in the ankle, but he knew his mother wouldn't like that. He thought about giving her a little poke in the stomach, but his mother wouldn't like that either. His mother wouldn't like anything he was thinking.

Sam stood glumly on the curb next to Mrs. High, watching the cars hurry past. He wished she would vanish in a puff of smoke, but she wasn't going to vanish. She was going to walk him across the street, and there was nothing he could do to stop her.

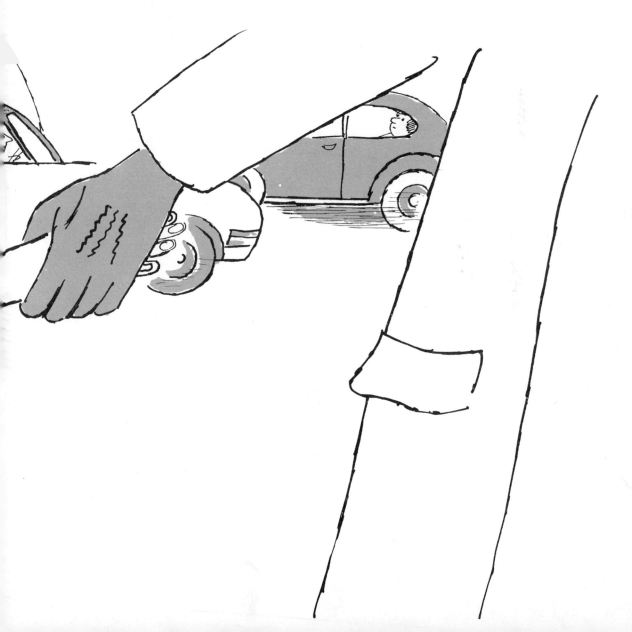

Whoosh! A car came rushing down Grant Street. It rushed through a puddle of rain and the water splattered—all over Sam and Mrs. High. Mrs. High squealed. She let go of Sam's hand, pulled a handkerchief out of her purse, and began to dab the water spots from her coat. Sam didn't care about water spots. He just stared at the red light, and hoped and hoped and hoped.

The light turned green.

An enormous smile stretched Sam's mouth from cheek to cheek. "See you later, Mrs. High," he said politely. Then quickly—but not *too* quickly—he looked up and down the street, stepped off the curb, and walked straight to the other side.

David was still waiting patiently on the stoop. "I'm sorry that I'm late," Sam said to David. "But it's a very long walk to your house, all by myself."

Rules For Safety When You Walk

1. Cross only at the corner of the street.
   Cross when the traffic light facing you is green.
   If there is no light or traffic officer, look both ways
   and cross when the road is clear.
   Walk fast, but do not run.

2. Stay on the curb as you wait for the light to change
   or for traffic to pass.

3. Do not turn back in the middle of the street.

4. Never dart into the street from between parked cars.

5. Never run into the street to chase a ball or a pet.

6. Don't let packages, hats, your umbrella, or your
   coat collar block your view.

7. Don't play in streets or alleys.

8. Choose the safe way from one place to another, even if it takes a little longer.

9. Do not accept rides from strangers.

10. If you must walk in the street, walk on the left side so that you can see the traffic coming toward you.

11. At night, be sure drivers can see you. Wear something white or carry a light.

12. Never argue with a moving car, even if the car is wrong and you are right.

13. Obey safety rules when you're with a group. Your safety is up to you, not your friends.